# Dear Parent:
## Your child's love of reading starts here!

Every child learns to read in a different way and at his or her own speed. Some go back and forth between reading levels and read favorite books again and again. Others read through each level in order. You can help your young reader improve and become more confident by encouraging his or her own interests and abilities. From books your child reads with you to the first books he or she reads alone, there are I Can Read Books for every stage of reading:

**SHARED READING**
Basic language, word repetition, and whimsical illustrations, ideal for sharing with your emergent reader

**BEGINNING READING**
Short sentences, familiar words, and simple concepts for children eager to read on their own

**READING WITH HELP**
Engaging stories, longer sentences, and language play for developing readers

**READING ALONE**
Complex plots, challenging vocabulary, and high-interest topics for the independent reader

I Can Read Books have introduced children to the joy of reading since 1957. Featuring award-winning authors and illustrators and a fabulous cast of beloved characters, I Can Read Books set the standard for beginning readers.

A lifetime of discovery begins with the magical words "I Can Read!"

*Visit www.icanread.com for information*
*on enriching your child's reading experience.*

I Can Read® and I Can Read Book® are trademarks of HarperCollins Publishers.
Pete the Kitty: Wash Your Hands
Text copyright © 2022 by Kimberly and James Dean
Illustrations copyright © 2022 by James Dean
Pete the Kitty © 2015 Pete the Cat, LLC
Pete the Kitty is a registered trademark of Pete the Cat, LLC, Registration Number 5576697

Library of Congress Control Number: 2021943588
ISBN 978-0-06-297418-1 (trade bdg.)—ISBN 978-0-06-297417-4 (pbk.)

Book design by Jeanne Hogle
21 22 23 24 25  LSCC  10 9 8 7 6 5 4 3 2 1  ❖  First Edition

My First SHARED READING

I Can Read!

# Pete the Kitty

## WASH YOUR HANDS

by Kimberly and James Dean

**HARPER**

*An Imprint of HarperCollinsPublishers*

"Wash your hands!"
says Mom.
"Okay!" says Pete the Kitty.

# Pete's hands are not clean!

"I'll help you," says Bob.
"Watch me!"

7

"Turn on the water,"
Bob says.

"Then wet your hands."

SPLISH!

"Scrub your hands with soap."

SCRUB! SCRUB! SCRUB!

"Rinse your hands
with water."
SPLASH!

"Then dry your hands."
RUB! RUB! RUB!

"Now you try it!"

Bob says.

SPLISH!

SCRUB!

SPLASH!

RUB!

"Ta-da!" says Pete

"Great job!" says Bob.

"We must wash our hands
many times a day," says Bob.
"When?" asks Pete.

Wash your hands
after you play.
SPLISH! SCRUB!
SPLASH! RUB!

Wash your hands
when you throw trash away.
SPLISH! SCRUB!
SPLASH! RUB!

Wash your hands
before you eat.
SPLISH! SCRUB!
SPLASH! RUB!

Wash your hands
after a treat.
SPLISH! SCRUB!
SPLASH! RUB!

Wash your hands
when someone is sick.
SPLISH! SCRUB!
SPLASH! RUB!

Wash your hands
if you just have to pick.
SPLISH! SCRUB!
SPLASH! RUB!

Wash your hands
if you sneeze, cough, or blow.
SPLISH! SCRUB!
SPLASH! RUB!

And please wash your hands
after you go!
SPLISH! SCRUB!
SPLASH! RUB!

"I've got it!" says Pete.

"Thank you, Bob!"

"Have fun!" Bob says.

SPLISH!

SCRUB!

SPLASH!

RUB!

"Did you wash your hands?"

Mom asks.

"Yes!" says Pete.

# Keeping clean is good!